sleepover Girls

Sleepover Girls is published by Stone Arch Books
A Capstone Imprint
1710 Roe Crest Drive
North Mankato, Minnesota 56003
www.capstonepub.com

Library of Congress Cataloging-in-Publication Data is available
on the Library of Congress website.
ISBN: 978-1-62370-260-1 (paperback)
ISBN: 978-1-4965-0540-8 (library binding)
ISBN: 978-1-62370-575-6 (eBook)
ISBN: 978-1-4965-2349-5 (eBook PDF)

Summary: Maren's mom is head-over-heels for her new boyfriend, but
Maren? Not so much. It's driving her nuts to see how much time they're
spending together. When she finds out they're getting married, Maren
is even more annoyed. Life is still somewhat bearable thanks to her
new improv comedy group and the Sleepover Girls, but everything is
changing too fast for Maren. Can Maren adjust to her new home life, or
will the stress be too much for her to deal with?

Designed by Alison Thiele

Illustrated by Paula Franco

Printed in the United States of America in Stevens Point, Wisconsin.
042015   008824WZF15

sleepover Girls

Maren's
NEW
FAMILY

by Jen Jones

STONE ARCH BOOKS
a capstone imprint

Maren Melissa Taylor

Maren is what you'd call "personality-plus" — sassy, bursting with energy, and always ready with a sharp one-liner. She dreams of becoming an actress or comedienne one day and moving to Hollywood to make it big. Not one to fuss over fashion, you'll often catch Maren wearing a hoodie over a sports tee and jeans. She is an only child, so she has adopted her friends as sisters.

Willow Marie Keys

Patient and kind, Willow is a wonderful
confidante and friend. (Just ask her twin,
Winston!) She is also a budding artist with
creativity for miles. She will definitely own
her own store one day, selling everything she
makes. Growing up in a hippie-esque family,
Willow acquired a Bohemian style that
perfectly suits her flower child within.

Delaney Ann Brand

Delaney's smart and motivated — and she's always on the go! Whether she's volunteering at the animal shelter or helping Maren with her homework, you can always count on Delaney. You'll usually spot low-maintenance Delaney in a ponytail and jeans (and don't forget her special charm bracelet, with unique charms to symbolize each one of the Sleepover Girls). She is a great role model for her younger sister, Gigi.

Ashley Francesca Maggio

Ashley is the baby of a lively Italian family.
Her older siblings (Josie, Roman, Gino, and Matt)
have taught her a lot, including how to get
attention in such a big family, which Ashley has
become a pro at. This fashionista-turned-blogger
is on top of every style trend and shares it with
the world via her blog, Magstar. Vivacious and
mischievous, Ashley is rarely sighted without
her beloved "purse puppy," Coco.

chapter One

"Maren!" came my mom's voice from downstairs for what seemed like the bazillionth time. Her voice was starting to get that tone, the one I knew meant I was skating on thin ice. "Time to grace us with your presence, please."

I knew I was in trouble, but I didn't care. I just pretended to be totally engrossed in the magazine I was reading, ignoring all the looks I was getting from my three best friends.

Never one to miss an opportunity to take charge, Delaney tapped her finger expectantly on her notepad.

"Time's up, Mar-Bear," she said, playfully throwing a pillow my way. "We've been holed up in your room for hours!"

"Yeah, I'm feeling a little trapped," said Ashley, looking up from the Instagram feed she was scrolling through on her phone. Ash was always finding new trends to blog about.

"We've got your back," Willow assured me, grabbing my hands. Reluctantly, I let her pull me off the bed.

As much as I hated to admit it, they were right. It was time to face the music and head downstairs, where my mom, her new boyfriend Gary (whom I'd secretly named "Garish," which means too bright or showy; it describes him perfectly), and his kids were waiting to start our "family" game night.

Thankfully, my mom said I could invite my friends since they were like family to me. That was the only thing keeping me sane right now.

I folded my arms and pouted like a little kid. "Do I really have to do this?" I whined. "My mom acts like we're all going to be an instant happy little family."

I knew I was being a brat, but it was bad enough that Garish seemed to be stealing away all of my mom's free time. Now his kids were coming over too? Clearly my mom and Garish were more serious than I thought.

"Don't you think you're being a bit dramatic about this?" asked Delaney. "We're just playing games, not sending your mom down the aisle or anything."

"Thank the stars for that," I said, leading the charge out of my room. "Let's do this."

Once we made it downstairs, I saw that my mom had put a lot of effort into game night. There was a Twister mat in place of our usual tablecloth, and she'd put Oreos on a checkerboard in place of the playing pieces. Plus, my mom had made funny little signs using Scrabble tiles to describe the food, like Candyland Pops for the cake pops and Pick-Up Stix for the candy-coated pretzel rods. If I wasn't so annoyed I would be impressed.

Watching the other girls "ooh" and "ahh" over my mom's decorating, I had a tiny pang of guilt. Usually, my mom and I would have had a blast brainstorming and setting everything up together. But I'd been avoiding her for days, pouting about the entire event.

"Celeste outdid herself this time, huh?" Garish said, grinning from ear to ear. His bald head seemed to be gleaming under the overhead light.

I nodded, smiled weakly, and stuffed a cake pop in my mouth to avoid making conversation.

Willow swooped in, hoping to lessen an awkward moment and ease the obvious tension.

"She sure did," she said, helping herself to a fruity Monopoly mocktail. "Ms. Taylor always knows how to get the party started! That must be where Maren gets it from."

My mom shot Willow a grateful look, then locked her eyes on me. "Maren, I think it's time you met Gary's children," she said, motioning toward the two kids play-fighting on the couch. They were dressed alike in some sort of striped nautical get-up. "This is Alice and Ace. They're in the second grade at Valley View Elementary."

As if it couldn't get any worse, they were twins! "Hi, guys," I said. "I didn't know they made matching outfits for boy-girl twins. How . . . cute."

Watching me struggle to be nice, Delaney stepped in to save the day. "Second grade? You might know my sister," she said to Alice and

Ace. "Gigi Brand? She's in fourth grade with Ms. Kirchner."

The twins kept right on tackling each other, as if they hadn't even heard Delaney. Garish cleared his throat, embarrassed. "Looks like they've still got plenty of energy to burn," he said. "So, on that note, who's ready to get their game on?"

My competitive spirit kicked in. "This girl," I said, raising my hand high. "As the reigning Trivial Pursuit champ, I believe I get to pick the first game. And that game is Pictionary!"

"Woo-hoo!" yelled Willow, always ready for anything that involved drawing or painting. She was a talented artist, so naturally, I snagged her for my team. Not so luckily, I also ended up with Garish and Alice. My mom, Ace, Delaney, and Ashley made up the other team.

While Garish set up the easel, my girls and I flopped onto our favorite spots on the sectional couch. My house was a second home to my friends. They'd slept over more times than I could ever try to count! It was part of our deal as the Sleepover Girls. Every Friday, we took turns hosting our weekly sleepovers. I lived for Fridays!

Ashley was up first at the easel, rocking flowered reading glasses for effect. "Dig in," my mom urged, passing the bowl full of drawing prompts at her. "First category: movie titles!"

Ash fished out her piece of paper and read it thoughtfully. She waited for Willow to turn the hourglass timer upside down. "And, go!" prompted Willow, chewing her long blond fishtail braid nervously.

Ashley eagerly started drawing something that kind of resembled an ice cube tray in a freezer. "*The Big Chill*!" guessed my mom, but Ashley shook her head. She pointed at the ice cube tray, trying to drive home the hint. The team kept throwing out ideas: *Ice Age*! *The Ice Storm*!

It seemed like time was going to run out, but Ace came through in the clutch. *"Frozen!"* he yelled just as the timer ran out. Ashley started jumping up and down at his correct answer.

"Nailed it!" she said, high-fiving him.

"She should have drawn Elsa," sniffed Alice, rolling her eyes. "Who draws an ice cube tray?"

I wasn't about to have this little girl trash-talking any of my friends, even if they were on the other team. "Why don't you see if you can do better?" I said, handing the bowl to her.

Alice took the challenge, digging deep into the bowl. "No problem," she said, straightening her striped sailor skirt. Once the timer started, she started drawing a girl with a tiara next to an open book (or at least it kind of looked like a book). It didn't take me long to decipher the clues.

"Princess Diaries," I yelled. "Bam!"

"Way to go, Maren," said Garish, smiling at me.

My happiness quickly faded. I looked the other way, only to find Alice doing a little victory dance and shaking her booty in my face. Charming! Avoiding my mom's stare, I cleared my throat and got up to hand the bowl to Delaney. "Your turn, D."

I may have been on Garish's team in the literal sense, but I was so not on Team Garish.

chapter Two

The game went on, until it finally came to my turn. I picked *Beauty and the Beast*, which would be easy. Once Ashley gave me the start signal, I started furiously drawing. I made a werewolf-like creature and a supermodel-slash-princess girl.

"*Teen Wolf!*" yelled Alice, bouncing up and down on the couch.

"Ummm, *Twilight*?" Willow guessed.

I shook my head no, drawing some extra beastly features and a castle for emphasis.

Garish seemed stumped, and the timer was going fast. Frustrated, I decided to go off the rails and just started pointing like crazy at my mom and Garish. Everyone just looked confused. Once the timer ran out, I heaved a big sigh and revealed, *"Beauty and the Beast!"*

My mom looked really mad, and I realized maybe I had gone too far. "I was just kidding," I started, but she got up and left the room. Garish ran after her, but not before he gave me a look of his own.

"Way to go, Maren," said Ace, ripping the sheet of paper off the easel, wadding it up, and lobbing it straight at my head. Before I could react, he and Alice stomped off in the same direction my mom and Garish had gone.

I figured the Sleepover Girls would be on my side, but even they seemed to think I'd crossed the line. Did no one have a sense of humor around here? Usually everyone appreciated my unique brand of comic relief.

"Was that really necessary?" Delaney asked, raising her eyebrows.

"You try having your house invaded by Garish and his twins," I huffed. "My mom and I were doing perfectly fine before they came into the picture."

And it was true! My mom and I were one of the tightest twosomes around. She and my dad had gotten divorced when I was little. After that, he'd moved from Valley View to San Diego (where I now have a pretty cool stepfamily whom I actually like).

Ever since my dad had left, my mom and I had been best friends. We'd traveled all over the world together, thanks to my mom's amazing job as editor of a popular travel magazine. Of course, now she'd probably be taking Garish instead of me on her fancy trips. Everything was changing, and I didn't like it.

Picking up on my sadness, Willow took pity on me. She went over and picked up the chocolate checkerboard. "Oreos always make everything better," she said, holding the board in front of me like a waitress. I shot her a grateful look and grabbed a handful.

"Why don't you go talk to her, Mar-Bear?" asked Ashley, grabbing an Oreo for herself. "You'll both feel better."

I didn't get the chance to make the first move, as my mom and Garish were standing in the doorway. Her arms were crossed, and she still looked upset.

"Maren, I think you owe Gary and the kids an apology," she said. Surveying the room, her face looked puzzled. "Where are Ace and Alice?"

As if on cue, Alice and Ace came bounding down the steps, their faces full of mischief.

"Nice house, Ms. Taylor," said Alice. "We just loved exploring it."

Ace tore through the room, stopping right in front of us four girls. "Yeah, who needs the *Princess Diaries* when you can just read Maren's diary?" He whipped out my journal and flashed it open at us, giggling like a crazy person.

My face flushed redder than my hair, and I shot out my seat to chase him around the room.

"How dare you?" I huffed, trying to grab it out of his grasp.

He jumped up on a chair and opened up my journal yet again. "I just love the part where you talk about wanting to kiss Winston," he said, striking a girly pose. I was beyond mortified!

Ashley looked like she was trying to smother a giggle, while a wide-eyed Willow clapped her hand over her mouth in shock. Winston was her twin, and though she and the girls had known he and I were kind of a "thing," I'm sure it was still weird to hear that I wanted to kiss her brother! (And unlike Alice and Ace, Winston and Willow were not evil twins!)

"Alice and Ace, I'm very disappointed in you," Garish said, stepping in before things got worse. "Give Maren her journal back right now, and then we're going home."

Ace jumped off the chair and reluctantly extended the journal, which I angrily snatched.

"Thanks for trying to make it a great evening, Celeste," said Garish, giving her a kiss on the cheek as she handed him his coat.

Alice and Ace dutifully stood by his side looking down at the floor, but the minute my mom and Garish weren't looking, Ace managed to stick his tongue out at me. I stuck my tongue out right back at him. I realized how childish it was, but I didn't care.

Once they were out the door, my mom's shoulders slumped in defeat. "Girls, I'm too tired to deal with cleaning up right now," she said. "Enjoy the rest of your sleepover. Maren, we'll talk in the morning."

Guilt trip, much? I guessed I kind of deserved it, though. The least I could do was clean up the game night stuff. The girls and I kicked into high gear, taking down the game supplies and food table in record speed. (I thought they didn't know what to say after the ridiculous way game night had gone down.)

Once everything was clean, I knew I needed to salvage the night. "Okay, we can't call it quits on game night without playing one more game," I said. "Who's down?"

Ashley's face spread into a smile. "I've got the perfect thing," she said, digging deep in her chevron-patterned overnight bag. She unearthed a pink box, and we all immediately started laughing.

"GIRL TALK!" we all screamed at once.

Girl Talk was a game Ashley's mom had played when she was a kid. She had kept it all these years and passed it down to Ashley. The idea was basically Truth or Dare in board game fashion, with "fortune cards" thrown in for good measure. Plus, there were these hilarious zit stickers that you had to wear if you messed up or refused to do something.

Willow was up first. She twirled the spinner with a flourish, and it landed on a dare: "Stand on one foot and balance a ruler on your chin for one minute."

Willow grabbed the remote control. "Will this work?" We all nodded and laughed as we watched Willow precariously perch the remote while balancing on one foot as we timed her.

"Success!" she said, triumphantly grabbing one of the fortune cards from the pile. "You will give birth to identical twins five days before your twenty-third birthday."

I swiped the card from her hand. "I think we've had enough twin talk for one night!" I grumbled. It was kind of funny, though, to think about Willow (who was a twin herself) being a mom to twins.

"Okay, my turn," I said, giving the spinner a whirl. Reading the dare to myself, I groaned loudly, prompting Delaney to snatch it and read it out loud.

"Call a radio station and dedicate a song to your crush," she said loudly.

My face flushed bright red yet again, and the other girls laughed at the reminder of my crush on Winston. "I think I'd rather risk breaking out than humiliate myself yet again this evening," I said, proudly placing a zit sticker smack dab on my nose.

I would rather have had ten real zits on my face than deal with Garish and his twins ever again.

chapter Three

Understandably, it took some time for the cold front at home to pass. My mom had been disappointed with my behavior at game night; plus, we'd already been on shaky ground before that. Not that my protest stopped her from spending any less time with Garish, of course. They were constantly together.

But I was still super surprised when I found Garish in our kitchen one morning.

"Good morning, Maren!" he said cheerfully. "I didn't realize you got up so early."

"My improv group is meeting before school," I stammered, not wanting to deal with him. I grabbed a banana and made my way back up to my room to get ready. Taking a deep breath, I went to grab my journal from the drawer when I noticed something on my nightstand. It was a plane ticket underneath a tacky plastic mini-version of the Hollywood sign.

"Pack your bags," said my mom, smiling from the doorway. "We're going to LA this weekend! Just me and you."

Say what? Now this was a welcome surprise and definitely an unexpected turn of events. I guessed my mom had finally forgiven me and decided to jet off on one of our signature whirlwind weekends.

"For real? This is incredible, Mom!" I said. "I think the closest I've ever gotten to LA was when Dad took me to Disneyland a few years back. Thank you!"

"Well, I think it's time we got out of this dreary, rainy weather and soaked in some sunshine," she said, her face brightening. "Plus, you and I could use a little alone time."

"Does this mean you forgive me for my terrible attitude?" I asked.

"I sure do," she said, smiling. "But I get the window seat." My mom and I were known to battle it out over the window, but she almost always let me have it. (This time? Probably not.)

I picked up the ticket and Hollywood sign souvenir, getting excited for what was to come. "Fair enough," I agreed. "Hollywood, here we come!"

After we declared a truce, it was almost impossible to sit through the rest of the week knowing what was in store for the weekend. So when our plane finally lowered toward the tarmac Friday night at the airport, I was like a kid in a candy store looking out at all of the lights. It was beautiful!

"Can we go see the Hollywood sign? Can we visit the wax museum? Can we go stalk Luke Lewis?" I bugged my mom, bouncing in my middle seat. (Yep, she got the window.)

My mom barely looked up from her reading. She was more than used to my hyper ways. "We're staying right on the Walk of Fame, so we'll do all of that," she assured me. "Well, maybe not stalk international superstar Luke Lewis. But if we have time, we can do one of those Star Homes tours."

I squealed in glee. That would be so much fun! Paparazzi for a day. Too bad you could only see the outside of the houses. Ashley would have loved for me to snap a shot of the massive walk-in closets, and I was sure Willow would have gone crazy over all of the expensive art pieces. Delaney, well, she'd probably have just wanted to snoop around and see how the stars really live. Oh well, seeing the outside was better than nothing.

I was beyond excited when our cab dropped us off at the Hollywood Roosevelt hotel, right in the thick of all of the Hollywood madness. I stepped out of our cab right onto one of the Walk of Fame stars lining the sidewalk! Even the sidewalk in LA was glittery.

"It's just like in the movies," I said with a happy sigh.

It was still pretty early in the evening, so we went exploring after we checked in. Hollywood Boulevard turned out to be a pretty insane place (in the best way). It was like a neon wonderland filled with tons of history and colorful characters!

We walked through the Ripley's Believe It or Not! Museum and the Dolby Theatre, where they do the Oscars every year. There were also tons of little souvenir shops, where I managed to snag little "Pup-arazzi" doggie T-shirts for Delaney's dog Frisco and Ashley's pup Coco. But my fave stop was Mann's Chinese Theatre, a decades-old movie theatre where lots of famous people had put their handprints and footprints in the concrete.

Once back at the hotel, I flipped on the TV and got ready for bed. Mom quietly excused herself into the bathroom and shut the door, probably so she could call Garish. Sure enough, soon I was able to make out the muffled sounds of my mom on the phone. (Her voice always had an extra spring in its step when she was talking to Garish.) I tried to concentrate on the TV screen, but instead I just found myself straining to hear what she was saying.

Finally, I hit "mute," just in time to hear her say, "Okay, well, I should go get some sleep. We've got a long day tomorrow. I love you."

The *L word*? Oh, no. This was WAY more serious than I thought.

chapter Four

Sure enough, I stayed up far too late, totally annoyed about my mom and Garish being in love. I knew it was selfish of me, but I didn't care. Needless to say, I wasn't thrilled when my mom rose bright and early.

"Rise and shine!" she said, nudging me awake. The clock read 7:45 a.m.

I groaned groggily. "Mom, it's the weekend!" I was used to sleeping in on Saturdays, especially because I was usually recovering from our all-nighter sleepovers. Plus, this was vacation. I didn't need any real-life roosters getting me out of bed before I was ready.

My mom was unimpressed. "Exactly, and we've only got a few days here, so hit the shower!" she directed.

Luckily, my mom had a fun day planned, and my grogginess was nothing a good breakfast couldn't fix. Once we were up and about, I was able to reset back to my happy place. We headed west with our rented convertible and ended up in Venice Beach, where the streets were lined with palm trees and people riding beach cruisers.

"Trust me, you're going to love it," said my mom, as she parked on a street called Electric Avenue.

We headed toward the beach boardwalk, which was packed with people and bustling with activity. I couldn't believe how many people were out this early in the morning! Hollywood Boulevard was nothing compared to this craziness! Neon-haired rollerbladers and skateboarders, street artists and musicians, henna tattoo artists, bohemian hippie types holding protest signs — this place had it all.

"Want to rent a tandem bike?" my mom asked as we passed a rental place. "We could go up toward Santa Monica." She motioned toward the Santa Monica Pier in the distance, where a giant Ferris wheel was spinning round and round.

It sounded fun, but I wanted to walk around and people-watch. "Let's grab some ice cream and explore first," I told her, bopping my head to the loud reggae music that filled the air. This place was unreal!

Cones in hand, we made our way down the boardwalk. My mom decided to get a henna tattoo on her hand, so I passed the time by poking around to find some more souvenirs for the Sleepover Girls. I found a miniature painting of the Pacific Ocean for Willow, a chunky turquoise bracelet for Ash, and a flashlight keychain for Delaney (she loves practical stuff!).

Once she was done, my mom flashed her henna tattoo proudly. It was pretty cool-looking, like lots of auburn vines were growing up her wrist.

As we started walking again, an orange hut with a beaded curtain caught my eye across the way. "Ooh, a palm reader!" I said, pointing toward the lighted sign shaped like a hand. "Mom, we have to do it."

She rolled her eyes, but a smile came over her face. "Your wish is this genie's command," she said, bowing and gesturing toward the hut. Inside we met a woman named Isis. She had a turban piled high on her head, a feather boa, and lots of bracelets going up her arms. She had a little table set up with a crystal ball and some tarot cards.

"Join me," she urged, patting the chair next to her. "To what do I owe the pleasure of a visit from such a ravishing redhead?"

I giggled and took the seat. "Um, I was hoping to get my palm read?"

"That would make sense," said Isis, smiling and taking my right hand to examine. "Mercy! You have a double heart line. Lucky you. You must have a very tight circle of friends." So far, this reading was pretty accurate!

Next, she had me cup my hand to make a C shape. "Your mercury mount is dominant," she mused, carefully examining the wrinkles. "This indicates that you're extremely talkative and that you also tend to dream big. I see you working in a creative field where you'll be able to impact lots of people."

Isis continued to assess my hand. "Mmmm, you have a major break in your life line," said Isis, tracing the curvy line that ran from my thumb to my wrist. She looked thoughtful. "That signals that a big change is going to happen in your life. We're talking earth-shattering. Huge."

I giggled. "Maybe I really will get discovered by an agent here in Hollywood," I joked, looking toward my mom to get her reaction.

But instead of laughing along with me, she just looked kind of pale. She seemed a little distracted for the rest of the reading and relieved once it was over.

Back out on the boardwalk, Mom seemed to bounce back a bit. "I'm starving," she said. "Want to go grab lunch?"

I never had to be talked into a tasty meal. "Sure!" I told her. "Let's find a sushi place. I'm in the mood for trying something new."

We found a place that had outdoor seating with a killer view of the water, and there was a fun steel-drum band playing just across the way. Looking out at the glimmering ocean, blinding blue sky, and colorful cast of characters, I had no doubt that this was the place I wanted to live someday. Everything just felt perfect.

But that perfect moment did not last long. As soon as our drinks came out and we ordered some sushi rolls, my mom seemed uneasy again. "Maren, we need to talk," she said, shifting a little bit in her seat.

I should have known. I was about to get a "talking-to" for how awful I'd been acting lately. Here my mom was, treating me to this awesome weekend, and I hadn't really earned such an amazing trip.

"Mom, you don't have to say it," I told her, fiddling with my chopsticks nervously. "I know I've been a brat lately. I'm so sorry."

"It's not that," my mom said. She grabbed her water and gulped it down. "I can understand why you'd be resistant to change, even if you haven't exactly been displaying model behavior lately. But the thing is, honey, I need you to understand that Gary and I are very serious. In fact, he's asked me to marry him."

I dropped the chopsticks, feeling paralyzed all of a sudden. Stars started dancing in front of my eyes, and my mom looked really blurry. I felt like I couldn't breathe. I shoved my chair back and ran out of the restaurant onto the beach. I kept running until I reached the water.

"Maren!" my mom called, coming after me. I waded into the water farther, letting it envelop the cuffs of my capris. I couldn't face her, not right now.

How could she do this to us? We were supposed to be the Dynamic Duo, and we'd always been just fine on our own. Now I was going to be stuck with a life sentence chained to Garish and his evil twins. This was not the happy ending I envisioned for my life.

chapter Five

"Okay, Portlandia Players, we're just a few weeks away from taking the stage for our big show," said our theater advisor, Ms. Green. "Who's ready to get started?"

Everyone started whooping and hollering, and Winston gave me a huge smile. A few weeks had passed since the dreamy-turned-disastrous trip to LA, and my improv club was the only thing keeping me sane (besides the Sleepover Girls, obviously). Things hadn't gone very well for the rest of our trip, or once we'd gotten back to Valley View, for that matter. I'd been avoiding my mom and Garish at all costs.

"Earth to Maren," said Ms. Green, snapping me out of my stupor. "Are you going to join us for a game of Yes, Let's! or do you need more time to thaw before the icebreaker?" Everyone else was standing and ready to go.

"Count me in," I told her, hustling to join them. "In fact, I'll go first! Let's all act like babies."

"YES! Let's all act like babies," everyone yelled in response.

Suddenly the room was filled with the sounds of fake crying, people crawling around on the floor, and other baby-like actions. We did that for a few minutes, until Winston yelled, "Let's hug it out!"

"YES! Let's hug it out," I answered loudly along with everyone else.

We all started hugging, acting like we hadn't seen each other in ages. My heart fluttered a little when I got my hug from Winston.

Before the exercise was over, we'd all dug holes with fake shovels, acted like chimpanzees, and had an imaginary tug of war.

"Let's finish this exercise!" yelled Ms. Green, giving us our cue that it was time to move on.

"YES! LET'S FINISH THIS EXERCISE!" we all screamed.

After we all settled down, Ms. Green explained the next exercise, which was called Puppeteer. Basically, she would read a story out loud while we acted it out in pairs (one person the puppeteer, the other the marionette). Winston shot me a sideways grin.

"Want to be partners?" he asked. "No *strings* attached."

I scoffed at his cheesy joke, but secretly I loved his sense of humor. "Deal," I said, offering my hand to shake on it. "I'll even let you be puppeteer, if you promise not to torture us next time we sleep over."

Winston was known for playing crazy pranks on us whenever we slept at his and Willow's house. (But for some reason, I continued to crush on him anyway.)

Winston pretended to consider my offer. "You drive a tough bargain," he said, pulling me up off the ground. "I'll shake on that, but I'm not promising anything beyond the next sleepover. I have a reputation to protect."

Franny Martin laughed from the other side of the room. "Aren't you two getting cozy?" she said loudly. "I guess not much has changed since our little campout."

Not too long ago, Franny and her twin Zoey had joined the Sleepover Girls for a backyard sleepover at Willow's, where I'd revealed my crush on Winston for the first time. And for about the millionth time, I found myself regretting the fact that she and Zoey were in on the secret.

"Focus, people!" Ms. Green urged us, clapping her hands to stop the commotion. "Improv is about working together as a team. And on that note, why don't we have Maren, Winston, Franny, and Grant go first and show us how it's done?"

We all got into position. Winston stood behind me, taking my wrists so he could maneuver me properly. Ms. Green launched into the "story."

"The school dance is tonight and Grant and Maren need to look their best! Time to get ready," Ms. Green said.

Winston took the cue and started moving my arms to make it look like I was putting on lipstick and fixing my hair. Franny did the same for Grant, except she lifted his arms to make muscles and flex them in the fake mirror. Everyone started giggling, which was good to hear.

"Time for Grant to pick up Maren for their date," prompted Ms. Green. Franny made Grant start the fake car and wheel his way over toward me. She took his hand and used it to open the imaginary door, and Winston plunked me into a seated position next to Grant.

Our "car" made its way over to the "dance," where Ms. Green read the next prompt. "Grant asks Maren to dance, but she's not up for it just yet."

Franny made Grant tap me on the shoulder, and Winston grabbed my face and shook it violently back and forth to say "No!" Franny then made Grant get down on his knees in a begging position, which made everyone laugh loudly again. Winston crossed my arms and turned me around so my back was to Grant.

Was it me, or was this turning into a bad music video? I was starting to feel a little flustered, which was weird. Usually I loved doing this kind of stuff.

Ms. Green kept going. "Grant finally wears Maren down, and she agrees to hit the dance floor and show off her stuff. Bust a move!"

Winston started moving my arms to make me do the "robot," which got a bunch of laughs. As he kept moving me every which way, I started to feel a little sick to my stomach and my face got really flushed. After a few minutes, I was having trouble breathing again — the same way I'd felt after my mom told me she was getting married. I was having a panic attack!

"Excuse me," I managed, breaking free of Winston's grip and running into the hallway. I leaned against one of the lockers, which felt especially cool against my flushed skin. I tried to catch my breath, but it wasn't easy.

"Maren?" Ms. Green peeked her head around the doorway. When she saw my condition, she came out of the classroom, shutting the door quietly behind her. "What's going on?"

My face was buried in my hands, but I peeked out to make sure Winston wasn't following her outside. She followed my gaze and gave me a reassuring smile. "Don't worry, they're still going strong with the exercise in there," she told me.

The tension in my shoulders released, and the tears started to flow. "I don't know what's wrong with me," I said.

"It seems like you are stressed about something," Ms. Green said.

"I guess I didn't realize how stressed I really am. I feel like I don't have control over anything in my life anymore," I told her.

Ms. Green looked concerned. "Why do you feel like you don't have control?"

It all came out in a rush — my mom getting engaged so quickly, the evil twins, my fears about losing my mom to Garish. It felt good to get it all out.

"That's a lot for one person to take on in a short time, Maren," she said, putting her hand on my shoulder. "Maybe you could try talking to one of the middle school guidance counselors. We could even bring in your mom and her fiancé so that you could talk about all the changes going on with someone who's removed from the situation."

I shuddered. Being locked up in a room and forced to talk about my feelings with Garish was not the way to fix this. But I didn't want to make Ms. Green feel bad, so I just muttered, "Maybe that would help."

But, at that point, I wasn't sure if anything could help.

chapter Six

Delaney, Ashley, and Willow were waiting on my doorstep when I got home from improv practice later that afternoon. Ms. Green had let me go early, probably to spare me the embarrassment of having to go back and face everyone after my meltdown.

Delaney thrust out a handful of colorful Gerbera daisies, followed by a jumbo bubble tea courtesy of Ashley.

"We heard you could use a few things to brighten your day," said Willow softly.

"Oh, boy, word travels fast," I said, shaking my head in embarrassment. "I guess Winston told you about my mini-meltdown at improv?"

Ashley flopped down on our porch swing. "Let's just say a little birdie told us, but we didn't exactly need anyone to tip us off," she said. "Ever since game night and your trip to LA, we've been pretty worried about you."

Delaney nodded, joining her on the swing. "Yeah, this is the least we can do," she added. "You know we're always here to listen. After all, we can't have our favorite redhead running off to Hollywood to live forever."

I started to tear up again. Usually I was all amped up after improv practice, but right then, I was an emotional wreck! A relaxing afternoon with the girls might be just what I needed. Unfortunately, my mom had other plans.

"Maren, you're home," said my mom, opening the door from inside. Her face looked worried. "I've been waiting for you. We need to talk. Sorry, girls, can you come back later or tomorrow?"

The girls looked bummed, but they nodded in understanding. "Sure, Ms. T," said Willow. "We just wanted to drop by and say hi to Maren."

"Call me later if you need to vent," Delaney whispered before she grabbed her helmet and took off on her pale blue bike.

My heart sunk as they pedaled away. Clearly the girls weren't the only ones who'd heard about my panic attack.

"Are you okay, Maren?" my mom asked. "Ms. Green called and said you were having some problems during improv today."

"I'm fine," I said, trying not to cry. I sure wasn't going to tell her what was wrong with Garish sitting there.

"Are you really?" my mom asked.

"Yes," I said. "There's just a lot going on. I'm fine, so please stop asking."

"It's time to get things out in the open, Maren," said Garish, taking my mom's hand from across the table. "You can't avoid me forever. Like it or not, we're going to be a family soon."

I gulped down a giant sip of bubble tea. "Like, how soon?" I managed to get out.

Garish and my mom exchanged a smile. "A few weeks from now," my mom said, beaming despite the somber mood in the room.

"A few weeks? Wow," I said, barely able to form words.

"We don't want anything fancy. In fact, we're actually going to take part in a big mass wedding ceremony downtown. Afterward, there will be a casual party. And you, of course, will be one of the guests of honor," she said.

Leave it to my mom to buck tradition. She jumped into everything in life headfirst, and apparently her second marriage was going to be no different.

I wasn't really sure what else to say, so I just sat there sipping my bubble tea. I tried to smile, but my face wouldn't cooperate.

My mom and Garish used my silence as an opportunity to launch into a lecture, talking about how happy they were together. They went on and on, throwing out keywords like *blended family* and *new beginnings*, but I'd pretty much tuned them out at that point.

It didn't really matter what I said anyway, since they had clearly mapped out our future without even asking what I thought.

My ears didn't perk up until my mom said, "So, we're going to need you to babysit Friday night. Gary has the twins this weekend, but we're going to head downtown to get our marriage license and do a celebratory dinner. It'll be a great opportunity for you to get to know Alice and Ace better before the big day."

Now that was a non-negotiable. Even if I wanted to babysit (which I definitely didn't), Fridays were sacred. "Mom, I'm supposed to sleep over at Ashley's Friday night!" I said, tearing up again. I hadn't missed one of our weekly sleepovers, well, ever. And I wasn't about to start now.

"The girls will understand," my mom said insistently. "This isn't up for debate."

I shot her a death glare and started plucking the petals off one of the Gerbera daisies. "Can I at least have the girls over to our house instead?" I begged. "They can help take care of Alice and Ace. Delaney's the star babysitter in her neighborhood."

To his credit, Garish relented first. "I don't see why not," he told my mom. "After all,

Delaney, Ashley, and Willow are practically like daughters to you. Alice and Ace might as well get to know their semi-sisters to be."

Okay, so he'd scored a few points with that one, but it was going to take a lot more to win me over.

"It's settled," I told my mom. "The Sleepover Girls will take care of the twins Friday night."

And that's exactly how it went down. The Sleepover Girls did not disappoint. In fact, they were even more prepared than I had hoped.

Delaney showed up first, toting a giant Lego set, puzzles, and a few other games. "I figure we can keep everyone out of trouble if we stay busy," she said.

Willow was next, bearing awesome matching friendship bracelets for the twins. "I've been hard at work on my Rainbow Loom," she said.

"I brought it with me in case we need another activity to do as a group."

And Ashley showed up with not only her dog, Coco, but also a giant pan of lasagna made with love by her über-Italian mom, Mrs. Maggio.

"Mamma mia!" I said, taking a whiff of Mrs. M's amazing spaghetti sauce. "How did I get so lucky to have such awesome friends?"

"It's the least my mom could do since we didn't end up hosting the sleepover," she said.

"I'd much rather be at your house," I assured her, petting Coco's head woefully. "Or just about anywhere but here."

My mom cleared her throat loudly from the other room. "I heard that," she said, coming in to join us. "Luckily, nothing you say can ruin my mood right now. I'm about to go get my marriage license!"

She did a little happy twirl, and for a second,

I actually shared her joy. I just wished her happiness didn't have to include bringing someone new into our lives who would change things forever.

chapter Seven

Mrs. Maggio always says, "Pasta brings people together," and so far, she was right. The twins had been pretty well behaved since Garish had dropped them off — mostly because they'd had their faces buried in lasagna. We'd all finished, but the twins were still going strong.

"This is *soooooo* good," said Alice, finishing off her last bite with a large string of cheese hanging between her mouth and the fork.

"Ashley, can we move in with you? My dad's cooking is totally gross."

The mention of the words "moving in" made me bristle; after all, the twins would be staying at our house every other weekend once Garish moved in and left his bachelor pad behind.

But Ashley just grinned. "Sure, but only if you like dogs. Coco here is queen of the house!" she said. She scooped up Coco, who promptly gave her a big lick on the nose.

Ace huffed. "Gross! You let her lick your face? That is disgusting."

Ashley's face darkened — no one messed with her precious puppy. (Even if Ace was kind of right.) But before she could retort, Willow stepped in to keep the peace.

"I hope everyone has room for ice cream!" she said. "It's sundae-making time!"

In true Willow form, she'd set up a glorious display on the counter, complete with sprinkles, various sauces, fruit, chopped nuts, and crumbled Oreos.

Pretty soon we all had sundaes piled high with all the toppings a girl (or guy) could want. I dug right in. After all, the more I stuffed my face, the less I had to make actual conversation with my future "siblings." Willow and Delaney picked up the slack, reminiscing with Alice and Ace about their Valley View elementary school memories and teachers they had in common.

"I'll never forget the way Ms. Laskey used to trill her *R*s," said Delaney, giggling at the memory. *"Darrrrlings*, take out your *arrrrrrt* supplies."

Alice giggled along with her. "She still does that!" she exclaimed.

Watching them trade stories, I almost felt a pang of hope. I'd always wanted a little sister. Maybe Alice and I could actually find a way to get along once everything settled down. But before I could even process my change of heart, Ace threw us all for a loop and started choking uncontrollably. His face turned really red and he couldn't stop!

"Ace!" I exclaimed, running over to him to pat his back. "Are you okay? Breathe!"

His eyes bulged out and got all watery, and he kept right on coughing. Alice took a look at his ice cream bowl and looked worried.

"He's got a peanut allergy!" she yelled. "Maren, how could you let him put those on his sundae?"

The allergy was news to me, but I didn't have time to worry about Alice blaming me. I had to make sure Ace didn't die!

"*Helllllp!*" he cried, falling to the floor and choking even more.

"What do we do?" cried Willow, clearly alarmed. Her voice was barely audible over Ace's loud coughing sounds. She knelt down next to him to try to comfort him and get him to stop choking.

Near tears, I snatched Ashley's phone off the table. "Call nine-one-one, then call Gary," I said authoritatively, starting to dial the numbers.

Ace hopped up, suddenly fine. "No need for that," he said, shooting Alice a mischievous look. Together, they said, "Gotcha!"

My worry turned into full-on rage. I should have known they weren't capable of acting like normal little kids. I opened my mouth to give them a healthy dose of Maren madness, but Ashley cut me off.

"Not cool, you guys," she told the twins. "Are you trying to give all of us a heart attack?"

Ace shrugged and stuffed a handful of peanuts in his mouth. "It's just a joke," he told us. "And you have to admit, I was pretty convincing."

"Oh, you were convincing," I told him, still super irritated. "I guess next time we'll just assume you're faking it and let you go on choking, even if it's not fake."

Willow tried to smooth the tension. "You guys totally got us," she admitted to the twins. "Very funny. I say we get out of the kitchen and go play with Legos or something. Who's down?"

Alice and Ace perked up. "Okay! Can we go play in our new room?"

My mood got even more grim at the mention of *their* new room. My mom was in the midst of redoing her home office to be a guest room for the twins, which made me kind of sad. Her office had always been so cool! It had a big leopard-print lounger, a disco ball, and a fuzzy shag rug, plus lots of pictures of her on her world travels over the years. Now all that was going to go away so it could be ground zero for the twins.

Delaney and Willow went upstairs to get the twins situated with their Legos, while I gladly stayed downstairs with Ashley. (Babysitting in fours had its perks! I'd have to do it this way more often, especially when the evil twins were involved.) Coco bounded up the steps after them, her fluffy tail bouncing in her wake.

"Coco!" Ashley called after her, but her dog was set on being part of the action.

"Let her go," I told Ash. "She'll love curling up on my mom's furry rug."

We decided to cue up a chick flick, and before we'd even finished with the credits, Delaney and Willow came back down to join us. "All's well on the Lego front," grinned Delaney.

I heaved a deep sigh, relieved that I wouldn't have to deal with them for a little while. Ash pressed play again, and pretty soon, I was swept up in the flick. About a half hour in, Ash pressed pause.

"Bathroom break," she told us. "Too much soda!"

"No prob," said Delaney. "It'll give me a few minutes to go make another sundae."

But before Delaney even got up, we heard a piercing scream coming from upstairs.

"You guys!" Ashley called, sounding panicked. We all went running to her rescue, and when we reached the office/bedroom, we found Ashley in tears.

Speechless, she pointed at Coco, who was cowering in the corner — with all of her hair shaved off! She looked like a lion with a giant mane on her head and no fur on the rest of her body. Poor Coco!

We all turned toward the culprits, Alice and Ace, for an explanation. "We found our dad's shaver in your bathroom, so we thought we'd give Coco a makeover," said Ace, prompting Alice to start giggling.

Ashley stomped over to the corner and scooped up Coco, who looked really scared.

"That's it!" I grumbled, grabbing Ashley's phone once again to call Garish. And this time, no way was I going to hang up. This was a real emergency.

chapter Eight

"Maren, it's time to start the invites," my mom called, pounding on my door. I'd been hiding away in my room ever since the girls had left earlier that morning (with a newly shorn Coco in tow). "Time to emerge from your cave. Gary and the kids will be here later to help, but we need to get everything ready now."

I rolled my eyes and begrudgingly opened the door to let her into my bedroom. "Mom, you know I have improv practice this morning," I reminded her. "I still need to get ready. Didn't I earn my keep babysitting last night?"

"It's not like you're a saint in this situation," my mom huffed. "Also, you're not the one who had to stop your engagement celebration dinner to come home."

My blood started boiling again. "So it's my fault that the twins don't know how to behave? Maybe you should try talking to your future husband about that."

My mom raised her eyebrows. "Watch your tone," she warned. "I expect you downstairs to help me in no more than five minutes." She kept talking, mostly to herself, "Why, oh why, did I decide to do DIY pop-up invites?" I couldn't remember the last time I saw her in such a sour mood.

"Paper crafts are definitely not my thing," she mumbled.

Reluctantly, I followed her command and went downstairs, where we prepped everything in silence. I gathered the supplies (scissors, a ruler, cardstock, glue, and a blunt knife) while my mom worked on addressing the envelopes. The silence was unbearable!

I wished things between me and my mom would be normal again. This entire wedding thing could have been so much fun, and I knew my friends would have loved to help with the invitations. But with all the tension and fighting around my house lately, everything was just a mess. Needless to say, I was relieved when I finally had the excuse to leave and go to my improv class.

"Looks like Winston's mom is here to pick me up," I said, peeking out the window. "Gotta bolt!"

My mom barely looked up from her guest list. She was clearly not impressed with me or the entire process of making her own invitations. "Be back by two," she muttered. "That's when we're starting to make these darn things."

Once at practice, Ms. Green didn't waste any time starting.

"Okay, we're going to practice creative storytelling today," she told us. "After all, storytelling ability is the basic building block of any great improv sketch, as is your ability to build on each others' words and ideas. So, let's tell a story!"

Grant Thompson was up first. "Once, there was a girl who had horrible stage fright," he started, pointing at me to go next.

I racked my brain. "She was so nervous that she had a full-on meltdown during rehearsal and ran out of the room like a big baby," I said, hoping everyone would recognize my thinly veiled acknowledgement of the crazy way I'd acted at our last practice. (I was still totally mortified.) Winston rewarded me with an understanding grin, so I gratefully pointed at him to go next.

"So she ran into the wardrobe closet to hide instead of showing up to rehearsal," said Winston, pointing at Taylor for her turn.

"And she used the clothes to dress up like a clown so no one would recognize her," Taylor continued, pointing at Ms. Green.

Ms. Green was game to play along. "But when she tried to escape with her disguise, a circus recruiter found her and convinced her to run away with the traveling circus."

Franny was up next. "So she hopped aboard the circus caravan and became BFFs with the bearded lady."

The story kept getting crazier and crazier, and ended with the star of the story overcoming her stage fright to become a flame-eating trapeze artist. Maybe that was my solution! I could just run away with the circus and become the master of ceremonies or something. Not likely . . .

Ms. Green took us through a few more scenarios and stories, and before we knew it, practice was coming to a close.

"So. Much. Fun!" said Taylor, coming up to me and slinging her backpack over her shoulder. "I think a bunch of us are going to hang out at my house. Wanna join?" She lowered her voice to a whisper. "And yes, Win's coming."

My mind immediately went to my mom. I'd promised to help prep all the invites and other craft projects that needed to get done today. If I didn't show up, I'd seriously be in the doghouse.

But speaking of dogs, I remembered what the evil twins had done to sweet Coco the night before. I had zero desire to spend the afternoon being tortured by them again. Decision made.

I gave Taylor a high-five. "Count me in."

chapter Nine

"Wakey, wakey," said Delaney, waving a warm, yummy-smelling cinnamon roll under my nose. "Time to get up. We've all been up for an hour already!"

Ashley piled on, jumping on top of me. "And you have a *looooong* day ahead of you, so no time to waste."

I buried my face in the pillow, feeling blinded by the bright light streaming in through Delaney's bedroom window.

"Don't remind me," I groaned. "More wedding preparations with Garish and the gang — how exciting!"

Even the mention of Garish was enough to make me want to sleep all day. It was the morning after our Friday sleepover, and I'd been looking forward to it even more than usual all week. My mom and I were barely on speaking terms since my no-show last Saturday, and things were especially tense around the house.

"I just can't deal with this anymore, Maren," she'd said, her eyes especially sad. "Let me know when you're ready to be happy for me and accept the person I love."

I was surprised she'd even let me come to Delaney's sleepover, but maybe she was just happy to get rid of me for a night.

Willow snatched the pillow away, snapping me out of my train of thought. "Actually, we're kidnapping you for the day," she said. "And you have absolutely zero choice in the matter. So, up and at 'em, Taylor!"

"Right. Like my mom will allow that," I told them. "I'm going to be in wedding jail all day. In case you've forgotten, it's just a week away and there's a lot to do."

Delaney grinned, taking a bite of the cinnamon roll. "Actually, your mom knows all about our grand plan," she told me. "So let's get at it!"

I managed to drag myself out of the sleeping bag, and before I knew it, I was in Mrs. Brand's car being chauffeured to the mall! Apparently our big day of fun included a little retail therapy.

"First stop, smoothie station," announced Willow.

I didn't need to look at the menu to order my usual. "I'll take the Blueberry Energy Boost, please," I told the cashier. I had a feeling I'd need all the extra energy I could get today!

Once everyone had fruity, fun concoctions in hand, we snagged a booth so we could fuel up before shopping the day away.

"So, Maren," Willow began, "consider this our wedding intervention. It's time you embraced the fact that your mom is starting a new life, and that you're going to be a big part of it!"

I put my head on the table. Delaney gently pulled my ponytail upward so I had to face them all again.

"No arguments," she insisted. "We don't want you to have any regrets about the way you treated your mom. Give us the next few hours to turn your frown upside down."

Ashley brightened. "And what better way to color your world happy than with new clothes?" she grinned. "Our first mission is to find you a fabulous frock to wear on the big day."

We made our way over to Mayfair, where Ash wasted no time rifling through the racks to find me some options. "What about this?" she said, holding up a brightly colored party dress that looked more her style than mine.

I shook my head. "Nah," I told her, instead picking up a black, boring gown that looked better suited for a funeral than a wedding. "This fits the mood much better, in my opinion."

Delaney snatched it out of my hand with a stern look. "Dressing room. Now," she instructed, draping the selections Ashley had picked out over my arm. My friends weren't messing around!

As I tried each of the dresses on, I couldn't help but think about my mom, who'd had to go shopping for her wedding dress all by herself. I did wish I'd been there for her more lately, but everything was just so overwhelming.

Willow knocked on the door, draping a flowing emerald green dress over the top of it. "I think I've found a winner," she told me, and as I held it up to my body in front of the mirror, I had to agree. I slowly walked out of the dressing room, feeling a little shy.

The deal was sealed when all of the girls saw me wearing it. "Totally gorgeous," said Ashley. "You just might upstage the bride!"

"Not possible," I told her. "My mom is going to look incredible. That's just how she rolls." No matter how annoyed I was with her, I couldn't deny that.

Delaney looked surprised and pleased. "Now that's the kind of attitude we like to see!" she said, putting her arm around me in approval. "And speaking of your mom, we're going to go spend a little time with her now that you've got your dress."

Willow patted her bag. "Yep, I've got my full bag of tricks here. We're going to help you guys make the party favors and place cards for the after-party," she told me.

I breathed a sigh of relief. Having the girls there would help provide a good buffer since my mom and I weren't exactly clicking right now. And, let's face it, with Willow leading the crafting charge, everything would look much more professional.

"Good deal," I told them. "But Ash, do you think you can be in the same room with Alice and Ace without strangling them?"

Ashley gave me a reassuring smile. "Anything for you, Mar-Bear," she said. "Besides, Coco's new look is starting to grow on me. It's like she's a doggie hipster or something. People are always stopping her on the street!" Leave it to Ashley to find a silver lining and turn her dog into a trendsetter.

And she kept her word, greeting the terrible twosome warmly once we got to my house, where there was already full-on DIY madness taking place. Scraps of paper, calligraphy pens, and other odds and ends seemed to be everywhere. There were also tons of mason jars and tiny succulent plants, which would soon become the party favors. Garish and the twins were stationed at the table, hard at work.

"You're just in time," my mom exclaimed. "We could use eight more hands to get all of this done!" Her hair was kind of messy, and she had dark circles under her eyes, but I could tell she was determined to cross the finish line.

Gary looked up from the place card he was creating. "Before we start, Alice and Ace have something for Ashley," he said, nudging Alice.

Alice looked sheepish. She pulled a glittery gift bag from under her chair. "Ashley, we're sorry about shaving Coco," said Ace.

Ashley rifled through the tissue paper and pulled out a cream-colored doggie puffer vest, just right for rainy Valley View days. "I love it," she told them.

Alice looked relieved. "We thought it might help keep her warm in this gross winter weather," she added. "Plus, it can hide that hideous haircut. Truce?"

Ashley shook Alice's and Ace's outstretched hands, which were a little dirty thanks to all the plants they'd been putting in the mason jars. "Absolutely," she told them. "And Coco's over it, too."

"What about you, Maren?" asked Alice. "Can you forgive us?"

Everyone looked at me expectantly, and it felt like I was in the hot seat. "Well, if you guys can agree to try for a clean slate, I see no reason why I can't, too," I said, trying to say the right thing. The weird thing was, I kind of meant it.

chapter Ten

Amid the sea of white veils and traditional wedding dresses, my mom definitely stood out in her polka-dotted purple vintage party dress and fluffy fascinator hat. She and Gary were holding hands amid the six hundred other couples who had gathered in the Portland Civic Center to take part in the My Big Fat West Coast Wedding event. The goal was to set the record for the biggest mass wedding ever to take place in the United States.

Alice, Ace, and I surrounded them as they stated their vows in unison with the other lovebirds. The fact that all of us could be so close together without strangling each other was definitely promising!

What a difference a week had made. We'd all spent lots of time together over the last seven days trying to get everything ready for today. They'd even come to support me at my improv showcase the night before, which was a pretty cool move considering all the other stuff going on and how terrible I had acted recently.

And I had to admit, having a few additional family members support me wasn't necessarily a bad thing. In fact, it felt amazing to have more fans.

After a few basic ceremonial things, the officiant clasped her hands together in excitement. "By the power vested in me by the state of Oregon, I now pronounce all of you joined in matrimony! You may kiss in celebration," she stated into the microphone.

The arena erupted in cheers as more than twelve hundred people made their marriages official at once. What a sight!

Gary dipped my mom and gave her a long kiss, prompting a few people nearby to burst into applause. I joined in, clapping along. Seeing the loving way they'd looked at each other during the ceremony made me realize how rude I was over the past few weeks. Not only was I rude, but selfish and immature as well. Thankfully my mom and Gary were able to look past my behavior and forgive me.

"Congratulations, Mrs. Willett," I told my mom sincerely once she came over to give me a hug.

"Thanks, honey," she said. "But I'll still be Ms. Taylor. Not everything needs to change."

Gary was next to hug me. I tried not to stiffen up and instead return the affection for my new stepdad. It was going to take some practice, but hopefully I'd get there. (I'd even started calling him by his real name when talking to my friends. I figured I'd better practice so I didn't slip up!)

"Thanks for giving us a chance, Maren," said Gary. "We're all in this adventure together, and I hope we can truly get along and build a trusting and loving family together."

"Sounds like a good plan," I told him. "It's the least I can do after being so difficult for so long. I promise I'm actually fun to be around — most of the time, anyway."

He grinned. "Well, we've got plenty of time to find out," he said. "But first, time to celebrate. Anyone else ready for a party?"

My mom whipped out her phone. "Wait, we can't leave without doing our first family picture," she said, tapping a fellow bride on the shoulder to ask her to do it. We all gathered together, the twins in their matching white outfits, Mom and Gary being all lovey-dovey, and me in the middle of it all. Kodak moment, indeed!

We joined the happy crowd leaving the arena and piled into Gary's minivan. We headed home to celebrate with our friends and family, and I couldn't wait to get the party started!

"Congratulations!" yelled the forty or so people gathered on our covered outdoor patio. Lively big band music was playing over our sound system, and guests were happily enjoying catered appetizers and a special drink called Love Potion #9.

The crepe paper chandeliers Willow had helped us make looked awesome flowing over the extra-long dinner table, which had lots of candles and flowers to set off the special place settings. And everyone seemed to love the favors we'd put together, which were succulent plants in mason jars with a little sign saying, "Let Love Grow."

All of the Sleepover Girls came running over at once when they saw me. "Look at you!" exclaimed Ashley. "Girl, that dress was made for you. All bow to the Emerald Queen."

"Thanks, but I think my mom is the only one who deserves queen status for today," I said, gesturing to my mom who was excitedly greeting some of our guests with Gary by her side.

Delaney grinned. "Aww, if I didn't know better, I would think you were actually coming around to this whole marriage thing," she joked. And they all knew me well enough to know that I actually was starting to accept

all of this, which was a relief to everyone —
especially my best friends and family.

When it was time for dinner to start, I took
the seat where the place card read, "Ms. Maren
Taylor." It was right next to my mom, who was
seated with Gary at the head of the table. Alice
and Ace were across from me on the other side,
right next to their dad.

"Speech! Speech! Speech!" one of my mom's
friends shouted over clinking glasses.

Before I could talk myself out of it, I stood
up to take on the challenge. My mom looked
surprised but thrilled and touched. I smoothed
my green dress self-consciously; for once, I
wasn't comfortable taking center stage.

"For as long as I can remember, it's been
just my mom and me," I said. "She's my hero,
my partner in crime, the one who keeps me in
line, and most importantly, my best friend. So,
naturally, I wasn't too thrilled when I heard

that someone else was treading on my turf." My throat caught, and I tried to blink back the tears that were threatening to escape.

"But now that I know Gary, and I see how happy he makes my mom, I've realized that three isn't a crowd," I said. "And that's because my mom has the biggest heart of anyone I know — and there's room for all of us in it." Now it was my mom's turn to wipe away a tear.

"So here's to a future filled with happiness, hope, and most importantly, family," I said, smiling across the table at my new stepfamily.

Everyone raised their glasses, and as we all toasted, I made eye contact with Delaney, Ashley, and Willow, too. After all, friends are the family you choose — and I'd chosen well. Cheers to that!

The Honesty Quiz

Maren wasn't always honest with her mom
(or her friends). Find out how honest you are
by adding up the points next to your answer.

1. Your BFF begs you to go with her to the new
   vampire flick that opens on Friday. You are
   SO over the vampire fad, so you:

   a) Sigh and say, "Count me in, Miss Dracula." (3)

   b) Smile and say, "Thanks, but no thanks! I simply
      can't stomach another vampire movie." (1)

   c) Tell a small lie and say you have to babysit
      your kid brother Friday night, even though
      your schedule is totally open. (2)

2. Your algebra teacher asks if you'd tutor some
   fourth graders with math, but being a math
   tutor is not your style. You:

   a) Admit that tutoring really isn't your thing. (1)

   b) Slyly cross your fingers and say you'd love to
      help, but you don't have enough time. (2)

   c) Open your planner and say, "Fine. When do
      we start?" (3)

3. When it comes to scoring deals on clothes, you and your friends are pros. But when a cashier zones out and forgets to scan a pair of leggings, you:

a) Pay for only what he charged you for and walk out of the store feeling lucky. You can't be blamed for his mistake, right? (3)

b) Strike up a lively conversation with him. If you can keep him talking, maybe he won't realize his mistake. (2)

c) Help the guy out and ask, "Did you scan all three leggings? I think you missed the purple pair." (1)

4. A friend invites you to a party at her house Friday night. Her parents are going out. You really want to go, but you know your parents' rule — no parties unless a parent is present. What do you do?

a) Talk to your dad about the party. When he asks if your friend's parents will be there, you say yes. You'll take your chances that he won't find out the truth. (2)

b) Tell your friend, "Thanks, but no thanks." Rules are rules. (1)

c) Tell your mom about the invite, but leave out the fact no parents will be there. If she doesn't ask, you won't tell. (3)

5. You catch your sister texting when she's supposed to be studying — again! You know her grades have been slipping. You decide to:

   a) Belt out, "BUSTED!" and dash off to tell your parents. Hey, she ratted you out last week, so she has it coming. (1)

   b) Offer to keep quiet in exchange for some cash for lunch tomorrow. (2)

   c) Roll your eyes, and ask how her homework is going. (3)

6. You're shopping for a school dance. Your friend tries on a skirt that she can barely zip and asks if it makes her look chubby. You:

   a) Shake your head and say, "Nope! If you like it, you should buy it." But actually, you're not sure it's a good look for her. (2)

   b) Look at the skirt closely and say, "I don't know." You don't want to hurt her feelings, but you don't want to encourage her to buy it, either. (3)

   c) Say, "It's not" very flattering, but if you like it . . ." (1)

7. The girls are going out for bubble tea tonight. Your mom said you could go — if your homework is done. Your book report is barely half-written. You:

a) Slam the book shut and declare, "Finished!" Your mom won't know the difference. Besides, you deserve a little fun after spending more than an hour with Huck Finn. (2)

b) Call your friends and explain the situation. Maybe they can get some tea to go for you. (1)

c) Beg and plead with your mom. Swear you are so close to being done. You'll finish it when you get home. (3)

8. A cute guy in your art class is no Picasso, but he tries so hard with every project. His latest mishap looks like he spilled a chicken burrito on his canvas. How do you react?

a) You aren't really sure what is going on with his painting. Is that a hamburger with a mustache? You just smile and nod in appreciation of his effort. (3)

b) You act sincere when you tell him, "You're amazing! I wish I was that creative." (2)

c) Take off your glasses, tilt your head, and squint. Then you shake your head and exclaim: "What is that?" (1)

9. One of the guys in your class got the answers to today's history quiz. You didn't read the chapter and can't believe there is going to be a quiz! You:

a) Know cheating is never okay. You let the teacher know the answers were leaked. (1)

b) Pretend you're sick, and spend history class in the school nurse's office. (3)

c) Ask your classmate for a copy of the answers. You'll read the chapter tonight. (2)

10. A potential babysitting client asks about your experience caring for babies under a year old. You have no experience. You respond:

a) "Kids that young are uncharted territory for me. But I'm willing to give it a shot." (1)

b) "I work with kids of all ages. Your little munchkin won't be a problem." (2)

c) "The tiny tikes are my specialty!" (3)

11. Panic! Your big report is due today. You thought you had another week to work on it. You quickly come up with a plan to handle the situation. You:

a) Tell your teacher you were going to print it, but your flash drive was missing from your locker. What kind of jerk breaks into lockers? (2)

b) Tell your teacher the truth. Everyone loses track of time once in a while. Maybe she'll give you a deadline extension. (1)

c) Tell your teacher you would really like one more weekend to finish it up. You were so fascinated by the subject that you are way over the word count. (3)

12. Game night with the family is more fun when you win. You're just two spots away from victory! On your roll, the dice tumble off the table. You look and see two threes. You say:

   a) "If they fell off the table, I get to roll again, right?" (3)

   b) "Ugh! Two threes!" (1)

   c) "Yes! I rolled snake eyes — just what I needed!" (2)

13. Your cheer squad's fund-raiser made twice as much cash as expected! But afterward you are exhausted and hungry. Five bucks could buy you a decent meal:

   a) But the money is the squad's, not yours. You bike home and make a sandwich. (1)

   b) But if the captain found out, you'd be off the squad for sure. Forget it! (3)

   c) And you did more than your share of the work. Next stop — lunch! (2)

14. The Environmental Club is pushing your school to go green. As a club member, you try to set an example at school. At home:

a) The trash can is way closer than the recycling bin. You are all about conserving your precious free time. (2)

b) No one in your family cares besides you, so why bother? Forcing them to recycle would needlessly ruffle feathers. (3)

c) It's the same deal. In fact, you set up a new bin and convince your family that recycling cans is worth the extra effort. (1)

15. Your band's bass player missed another practice. You know he's been busy helping out at home since his Army dad deployed. But it has been more than a month since you all played. And your friend could really use the practice. You:

a) Suggest he reconsider his commitment to the band for now. His family should take priority. The band will welcome him back when things slow down. (1)

b) Know he needs some motivation to get him going again. You tell him you heard the drummer suggested kicking him out of the band unless he comes to practice. (2)

c) Tell him the band has no talent without him. His skills are the foundation. A compliment will boost his ego. Hopefully that will inspire him to come to practice more often. (3)

14 to 23 points: You tell the truth no matter what. Your friends know you don't pull any punches — ever. Of course, there are times when a little discretion would go a long way. This doesn't mean stretching the truth. It just means using a little tact. It takes real skill to gently deliver a potentially painful, honest message. And sometimes it's better not to say anything than to be brutally honest.

24 to 22 points: You look out for yourself at all times. If a small fib or two keeps you out of trouble, you usually think it's worth it. You are pretty good at using words to get what you want — even if that means stretching the truth a little. However, your friendships could be so much deeper and more meaningful if you were more honest. It is priceless to trust your friends with the truth, even if they might not like it.

34 to 42 points: You value honesty. You really do. But you also value keeping drama to a minimum and pleasing your friends. You are the peacekeeper in your group. Unfortunately, that means that you are sometimes unhappy with your situation. Dealing with conflict is not your strength. But it's something you'll be doing your whole life. Speaking up for yourself and telling the truth take guts. It's not always easy, but it's important.

Note: This text was taken from *How Honest Are You?* by Jeni Wittrock (Capstone Press, 2012).

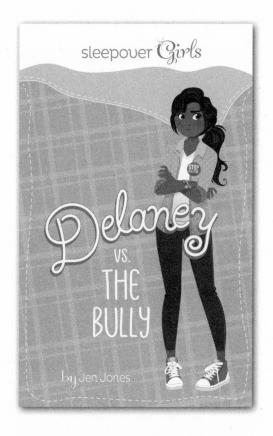

Can't get enough Sleepover Girls?
Check out the first chapter of

Delaney vs. the Bully

chapter One

"I can see it now: Delaney Brand — a new brand of leader," said Ashley, skywriting the words in the air as if on an invisible billboard. It was way after midnight, and we were all a little overtired and extra giddy.

Never one to be outdone, Maren jumped to her feet. "America's number-one brand — Delaney!" she said, making a big flourish with her hands for emphasis.

Willow giggled, looking up from the cute braided bracelet she was making for Ashley. "Delaney — a *brand* you can count on!"

Pretty soon we were all one-upping each other with more brand-related slogans for my pretend political campaign. Each slogan and idea was more outrageous than the next. I'd never thought much about my last name until tonight. I was pleasantly surprised by its potential.

"You guys are too much," I said. "If I ever do run for office, I'll be sure to hire you as my marketing team."

Maren reached for a pretzel and flopped onto her polka-dot comforter. "*If,* Laney?" she asked. "Try *when*. We all know it's only a matter of time till you're student council president."

Now that had a dreamy ring to it! I had to admit that she had a point. Ever since we'd gotten to middle school, I'd thrown myself into a bazillion different activities. Student council was my most recent conquest. What could I say? I was a joiner.

"Well, when that happens, I'm going to lobby for early dismissal on Fridays," I joked. "After all, don't they know we've got sleepovers to attend?"

Admittedly, there weren't many people at school who didn't know about our weekly sleepovers. After all, we'd been doing them for what felt like ages — but had really been since about third grade.

It first became a tradition thanks to my mom. She offered to watch Maren on weekends when her mom was jet setting on trips for her job. (Ahh, the fabulous life of a travel magazine editor!) One night, Maren's mom returned the favor, allowing Maren and me to each invite one other person. We invited Ashley and Willow. And that's how the Sleepover Girls (as we so originally nicknamed ourselves) were born! Every Friday night we embarked on yet another overnight adventure. We missed an occasional Friday, but it was very rare.

And here we were at Maren's — the place where it all started! I hugged Maren's fuzzy pillow a little closer just thinking about it.

"Earth to Delaney," yelled Maren, poking me in the arm with a pretzel rod. "Salted caramel ice cream is calling our names." Apparently the other girls had been planning a trip downstairs to raid the refrigerator while I'd been taking a trip down memory lane.

We tiptoed downstairs, trying not to wake Maren's mom. (She was still jet-lagged after a recent trip to Chile.) Luckily, she'd found time to go grocery shopping before our sleepover.

The kitchen was full of tasty treats to satisfy our cravings for midnight munchies. There were even a few souvenir snacks she'd brought back from her travels! Ash eagerly dipped her hand into a bag of beef jerky and thrust it out toward us. "Anyone?"

"I'll pass," Willow said, opting for a scoop of ice cream instead. "I'm doing the no-meat thing, remember?" A big animal lover, she'd recently decided to go vegetarian.

"Totally spaced on that, Wills! Props to you for vegging out," Ash said.

Maren stuck her spoon straight into the carton of ice cream and twirled it around. "I think we'll all be tempted to go veggie after the dissection unit coming up in science," she said. "So gross!"

"Even I think it's gross, and I love science," I said. "It's the one part of science class that I dread. But at least Willow and I can tackle it together!" Thankfully, I had Willow as my lab partner to help me navigate the amazing internal organs of dead animals.

"Oh yeah, I've been meaning to talk to you about that, Delaney," Willow said, nervously reaching for another spoonful of ice cream. "I actually got Mr. Tanner to agree to let me do an independent study instead of the dissection assignments. I just can't go there. I love animals too much. I hope you understand."

"I totally get it," I assured her. "But I'm still bummed. What will I do without my partner in crime?"

Ashley handed me a beef jerky stick in consolation. "Just join me and Sophie! There's already one group of three, so I don't see why Mr. Tanner wouldn't let you," she said.

It was the only class I had with both Ashley and Willow, which — coupled with the fact that I loved science — made it my favorite hour of the school day. (Having Maren in the class would have made it too perfect, but a girl could always dream.) The thought of joining their group made me feel way better. Here's hoping our teacher would allow it!

"Sounds like a plan," I said, eager to change the subject so Willow wouldn't feel bad. "Now who's up for watching a DVD?" We were known to fall asleep in front of the TV watching bad horror movies and cheesy chick flicks.

Maren giggled. "I was hoping someone would ask that. Hold that thought!" she said, running over to the counter and grabbing a tote bag. She pulled a pair of 3-D glasses out and put them on. "May I present to you . . . *Zombie Homecoming Queens* in full three-D action!"

Grabbing the DVD, she started walking zombie-style with her arms outstretched toward Ashley, who promptly shrieked and playfully swatted her away.

"Now that sounds delightfully bad," I said. "Bring on the flesh-eating frenzy."

Four BEST FRIENDS plus one weekly tradition equals a whole lot of FUN!

Join in by following Delaney, Maren, Ashley, and Willow's adventures in the Sleepover Girls series. Every Friday, new memories are made as these sixth-grade girls gather together for crafts, fashion, cooking, and of course girl talk! Grab your pillow, settle in, and get to know the Sleepover Girls.

sleepover Girls

Ashley GOES VIRAL

by Jen Jones

sleepover Girls

Delaney vs. THE BULLY

by Jen Jones

sleepover Girls

DOG DAYS for Delaney

by Jen Jones

sleepover Girls

Maren LOVES LUKE LEWIS

by Jen Jones

sleepover Girls

Maren's NEW FAMILY

by Jen Jones

sleepover Girls

The NEW Ashley

by Jen Jones

sleepover Girls

Willow's BOY-CRAZY BIRTHDAY

by Jen Jones

sleepover Girls

Willow's SPRING BREAK ADVENTURE

by Jen Jones

Want to throw a sleepover party your friends will never forget?

Let the Sleepover Girls help!
The Sleepover Girls Craft titles
are filled with easy recipes, crafts,
and other how-tos combined with
step-by-step instructions and colorful
photos that will help you throw the best
sleepover party ever! Grab all eight of
the Sleepover Girls Craft titles before
your next party so you can create
unforgettable memories.

sleepover Girls crafts

Amazing
OUTDOOR
ART
You Can Make
and Share

sleepover Girls crafts

Awesome
RECIPES
You Can Make and Share

sleepover Girls crafts

Colorful
CREATIONS
You Can Make and Share

sleepover Girls crafts

Fab
FASHIONS
You Can Make and Share

sleepover Girls crafts

Paper
PRESENTS
You Can Make and Share

sleepover Girls crafts

Spa
PROJECTS
You Can Make and Share

sleepover Girls crafts

Super
SCIENCE PROJECTS
You Can Make and Share

sleepover Girls crafts

Unique
ACCESSORIES
You Can Make and Share

About the Author: Jen Jones

Los Angeles-based author and journalist Jen Jones speaks fluent tween. She has written more than seventy books about celebrities, crafting, cheerleading, fashion, and just about any other obsession a girl in middle school could have — including her popular *Team Cheer!* and *Sleepover Girls* series for Capstone.

About the Illustrator:
Paula Franco

Paula was born and raised in Argentina. She studied Illustration, animation, and graphic design at Instituto Superior de Comunicacion Visual in Rosario, Argentina. After graduating, Paula moved to Italy for two years to learn more about illustration. Paula now lives in Argentina and works as a full-time illustrator. Her work is published worldwide. She spends a lot of her free time wandering around bookshops and playing with her rescued dogs.